MURDER IN MICHIGAN

RAMBLING RV COZY MYSTERIES, BOOK 1

PATTI BENNING

D1528372

SUMMER PRESCOTT BOOKS PUBLISHING

CHAPTER ONE

"Will that be all?"

Tulia looked at the small pile of diet pop and snacks on the counter, then glanced over at the advertisement for the lottery. The statewide drawing was up to eighty-six million dollars, a number that seemed as far away from her as the moon. She shrugged.

"I'll take a lottery ticket too, I guess. Why not? I'm feeling lucky today."

She left the gas station a few minutes later, already sipping one of the pops, with her lottery ticket tucked into the pocket of her sweatshirt. It was three in the afternoon, and she felt wonderfully free. The restaurant where she worked as a waitress had just had a huge grease fire in the kitchen an hour before, and the entire waitstaff had been let go for the rest of the day while the owners got it cleaned up. Sure, she was missing out on some tips, but it was Tuesday evening, and the restaurant had been slow anyway. An unexpected afternoon off was worth a few crumpled fives she would never see.

She dropped the bag containing her snacks and the pop she'd picked up for Luis on the passenger seat, then started her car and pulled onto the street. The sun was shining, the spring leaves were waving in the breeze, and she had all afternoon to do whatever she wanted, at least until Luis got home. She was sure he'd want to watch TV—there was a new show about Vikings he was obsessed with—but he would be at work until seven, which left her plenty of time to hang out with her best friend and keep looking for better jobs online.

There was an open parking spot right in front of her apartment when she pulled into the complex, and she hummed cheerfully as she got her things out of the car. It really was her lucky day. Maybe that lottery ticket would come to something after all. She pressed a button on her phone and spoke into it as she walked into the apartment building. "Remind me, check the lottery drawing at eight."

"Reminder set for—"

Satisfied, she shoved her phone back into her

purse and fished out her keys as she walked up the stairs. A wolf whistle greeted her when she unlocked the door, and she turned toward the culprit.

"Cicero! I'm back early, buddy. It's a nice surprise, huh? It was for me too."

Cicero ran his beak across the bars of his cage and let out another low whistle. He was her best friend, and in every way that mattered, was family. Just like her, he was thirty years old. Her parents had bought him when she was six months old. His hatch date was the day before her birthday, and they joked that he was her older brother. She'd been his person since she was old enough to walk, and he had come with her as soon as she rented her first apartment after her freshman year of college.

Cicero was an African grey parrot, and Tulia couldn't remember a time when he hadn't been right beside her, whistling and chattering away. With luck, she'd have another twenty or thirty years with him; African greys could live up to sixty years in captivity.

Now, she opened his cage door and let him climb on top as she put her purse and the bag of snacks on the small table in their cramped dining room. She shot a dirty glare at the electric keyboard Luis had insisted on buying, even though he couldn't play it without the neighbors getting upset and it took up space they could have used for a bigger table, then turned back to her bird when he spoke a single word in a man's voice.

"Lucy."

"We don't know anyone named Lucy, bud. Where on earth did you pick that up? It's been months, and we still don't know any Lucys." She tapped her chest. "Why won't you say my name? Tulia." She sounded it out for him, something she'd done since she was a little kid. Cicero could talk up a storm, but in all his years, he hadn't said her name once. If he ever did, she was pretty sure she would be crying happy tears for a year.

He let out another whistle, then repeated himself. "Lucy. Shut up."

She frowned at that last phrase. She'd have to talk to Luis again about what he said around Cicero. She didn't care how annoying his high-pitched whistles could get; Luis had better be nice to her buddy while she wasn't around.

"I swear, if this apartment is haunted by a ghost named Lucy, I'm gonna—" She broke off midsentence at the sound of a woman's voice coming from down the hall that led to her bedroom. Her blood ran cold. She had been joking about the ghost, but for a crazy moment, she thought she'd summoned something supernatural. Then, she heard the low murmur of a man's voice and felt as if her body had turned to a block of ice for another reason.

Luis wouldn't— She inhaled sharply at the unmistakable sound of a woman's giggle. No, he wouldn't cheat. He was supposed to be at work. There had to be some explanation…

Unable to hear anything but her rushing pulse and the quiet sounds of conversation coming from behind the bedroom door, she staggered down the hallway. It seemed longer than usual, the shadows darker. Her mind grasped futilely for other explanations but came up blank.

Then, her hand was on the doorknob, and she couldn't move. She could make out Luis's voice now, could have made out the words he was saying, but for the rushing in her ears. A woman responded, laughing, and for a moment, Tulia thought she might vomit all over the hall carpet.

Instead, she turned the doorknob and pushed the door open.

Part of her had been expecting them to fall silent, to turn and stare at her as the realization that she had uncovered their secret dawned on them, but this wasn't a movie. There was no dramatic moment. Instead, the woman who was sitting on the corner of *her* bed screamed and leapt up. Luis swore and fell off the other side of the bed, then clambered to his feet and started saying her name over and over again.

"Tulia, this isn't what it looks like. I swear, Tulia. Tulia…"

She ignored him, staring at the woman. She was younger, in her early twenties, with red hair and wide blue eyes that darted back and forth between her and Luis. Her mouth opened and closed silently, but she was pretty enough that it didn't make her look like a fish. Tulia hated her for it.

"Get out of my apartment."

Somehow, her voice was calm. The woman gaped, and instead of scurrying away in terror, she grabbed a pillow and started hitting Luis with it.

"You're a liar! A pig! You said you lived alone. *You said you were single!"*

Luis ducked and covered his head, and Tulia just stood there, watching. She didn't feel … anything. The ice in her veins had faded away to numbness.

Finally, the woman tossed the pillow at Luis with a last shout, turned, and hurried down the hall past her, her pretty blue eyes blinking tears away. She paused just past Tulia and turned to meet her eyes. "I'm so sorry. I didn't know; I swear."

"Just go." Tulia didn't care. She just didn't want to see the woman ever again.

Sniffling, the woman grabbed her purse from the couch—how had Tulia missed that?—and left the apartment, slamming the door behind her. Tulia stared at Luis.

"Really, Tulia, it was an accident."

"Leave." She pointed to the door. "Go. Now."

"I didn't mean to—she looks so much like you."

"She's a redhead. She has blue eyes."

"She's a natural blonde! You have to believe me, Tulia, I didn't mean to—"

She stomped into the room and stopped in front of him, her hands on her hips. "Really, Luis? It was an *accident?* How does that work? Did you mistake her for me because we look *oh so much* alike?"

"Ye— "He must have spotted the look on her face because he didn't finish the word. "No, of course not. I made a mistake, and I'll admit that. It's just, you work so much, and she started flirting with me, and I just wasn't thinking. This is the first time it happened; I swear."

She huffed. "Really? What's her name, Luis?"

"Lucy—" He shut his mouth with a clack of his teeth, but it was too late. Figuring Lucy had the right idea, she picked up the pillow and smacked him with it.

"It's been *months*. Cicero's been saying her name for *months*. Get out of my apartment! I never want to see you again!"

He scrambled to grab his things, and as soon as he was in the hallway, she slammed the apartment door shut in his face. Then, she turned and heaved the keyboard over, glad that it was on wheels. Opening the door, she ignored him as she shoved the device out, letting it tip over in the hallway. He had to scramble backward to keep his toes from getting crushed.

"And take your stupid keyboard with you. We're done. Done!"

She slammed the door again and turned the deadbolt this time before staggering over to the couch and collapsing in a heap of tears. Above her head, Cicero said, "Lucy!"

"Please, Cicero, not now." It was the last thing she said before she let the sobs overtake her.

It was getting dark outside by the time she stopped crying and made her way to the bathroom to wash her face. She stared at herself in the mirror, taking in her blotchy cheeks and red, puffy eyes. She wasn't a pretty crier but didn't think she was bad looking when she wasn't crying, which was most of the time. She had hazel eyes and hair that was dark blonde in the winter, but turned a lighter, pale shade at the slightest hint of sun. Her nose was perky in a cute sort of way, or so she'd always thought, and she kept herself in decent shape, though all the free food she got at the restaurant had given her a bit of a muffin top over the past year. But still, she wasn't *ugly*, or at least, she didn't think she was. Was she missing something? Was something wrong with her? Was she a terrible girlfriend? Luis was the one who had cheated, and she'd never take him back, not in a million years, but still, she couldn't help but feel like maybe, if she had been better, prettier, funnier … this wouldn't have happened.

She stared at herself until Cicero whistled, then went to give him dinner. She wasn't hungry. After turning off the lights, she settled down on the couch and pulled the throw blanket up to her chin. She wouldn't be able to sleep in her bed again until she washed *everything.* Staring at the dark ceiling, she wondered how to fix her life. Luis's cheating was just the tip of the iceberg. She wasn't happy and hadn't been for a long time. She wanted more, but what more was there? She was a thirty-year-old waitress with a bachelor's degree in English, a cheating *ex*-boyfriend, and no real prospects to speak of.

Turning onto her side, she closed her eyes. Life would get better. It had to. And if it didn't, well, maybe she and Cicero could just run away and live out of her car for a while. She'd always wanted to travel.

She woke up to a chirping sound coming from her cell phone. For a moment, she stared at the pattern on the couch, confused as to why she was sleeping out here and why her head felt like someone had blown a balloon up in it, but then she remembered what had happened the evening before. Groaning, she rolled over to silence her phone. Had she set an alarm? She didn't remember setting an alarm.

She turned the screen on and read the notification she'd set the evening before, reminding her to check the lottery drawing. Her phone must have set it for eight a.m. rather than eight p.m. Buying the lottery ticket seemed stupid now, but she sat up and navigated to the lottery website anyway. Taking the crinkled ticket out of her sweatshirt pocket—she hadn't had the energy to change into her pajamas the night before—she compared the numbers to the ones from the draw the night before. Then, she compared them again. Then, she pinched herself and compared them a third time.

Her hands shaking, she laid the ticket very carefully on the coffee table and found the lottery office's number on their website. The call seemed to take forever to ring through. Finally, someone answered, and Tulia spoke, her voice hoarse from crying the night before.

"Hello, my name is Tulia Blake, and I think I won the jackpot drawing from last night."

CHAPTER TWO

Two months later, Tulia was still in a state of shock, though it had faded slightly to be replaced by giddiness and a vague, spiteful glee. Sometimes she still lay awake at night, crying over what Luis had done, but most of the time, she kept those feelings at bay by imagining how livid he would be when he found out she'd won the lottery, and he'd missed out on his chance to share in the windfall by less than a day.

She hadn't told anyone yet, other than her parents. It felt strange keeping such a big secret from her friends, but one of the employees at the lottery office had taken pity on her when she admitted she had no idea what to do with so much money and had given her some advice.

Don't tell *anyone*, and get a financial advisor as soon as you walk out the door.

She'd played fast and loose with the advice since she'd told her parents and then had asked for her dad's help with finding the financial advisor, but she couldn't imagine keeping the truth about her winnings from *them*. She trusted them completely. One of the first things she'd done, before she even had the money in her bank account, was to offer to pay off their mortgage. They'd turned her down, but she was going to keep working on them. If anyone deserved a share of her lottery winnings, it was them.

Sometimes, when she woke up in the middle of the night, sure it was all just a dream, she opened her various bank accounts and investment reports—all of which her financial advisor had set up; his aid, along with the spending advice he'd given her, had proven invaluable—and just stared. Taxes had taken a good chunk out of the original eighty-six million, of course, but that left a bit over sixty million for her. It was a number that hadn't felt real when she heard it. It still didn't, even after she'd quit her job and gone on a moderate spending spree. The numbers in her accounts just didn't go *down*.

She was glad she'd gotten advice since she was in way over her head. Her first, mad impulse had been to buy a plane—never mind that she didn't know how to fly one. She'd also wanted to buy a mansion and give generous gifts to all her friends and family, which was probably the first instinct a lot of lottery winners had. Her financial advisor—and her parents—had encouraged her to sit down and really think about what she wanted to do.

She had, and she'd landed on doing the one thing she'd always wanted to do. Travel. See the world, or at least the country. She still didn't know what she wanted to do after that, but she had time to decide. A lot of the urgency she'd felt in her life seemed to have vanished along with all her stress about paying the bills.

And now she was looking at her brand spanking new RV, her hands on her hips as her father looked it over critically. It was grey and blue and was so new it felt like driving a spaceship. The interior was nicer than her apartment on such a scale that it almost didn't seem fair comparing them. Her little beige sedan, which was hooked up behind it, looked sad by comparison. So much was changing in her life, though, that she just hadn't been able to bring herself to sell it.

"I suppose it'll do," her father said at last, patting the side of the RV. Tulia exchanged an amused look with her mother. The RV cost more than their house—probably more than half the houses on their street combined. It was the most expensive thing anyone in her entire family had ever bought, and the one major treat she was giving herself until she was ready to buy a house—a reasonable house, and not a mansion, because she really didn't need thirty rooms and a helipad.

"You'll be safe, won't you, sweetie?" her mom asked once her father had given the RV his mark of approval. "Carry your pepper spray and remember to listen to your gut. If you feel like something is wrong, listen to that feeling."

"I'll be fine, Mom." She embraced her mother, then turned to her father, who was looking at her with a complicated expression.

"I'm so proud of you, sweetheart."

"I didn't do anything but buy a lottery ticket," she pointed out.

He clasped her shoulder. "I'm proud of you for going out there and chasing your dreams. Have a good time. And remember, if you need anything, your mother and I are just a phone call away."

She laughed, hugging him. "I think you said the same thing back when I first moved out. I'll be fine, it's just a road trip. I'll send you guys' pictures, and I'll let you know if I decide to change my itinerary."

She'd mapped out her route over the last two weeks with the help of a couple of friends, who knew she was going on a road trip but didn't know the truth about how she was funding it. She was planning to circle the entire United States before coming back to Michigan. It had been tempting to just take off without a plan, but common sense told her it would be safer for her friends and family to have at least a rough idea of where she'd be in case she dropped off the face of the world unexpectedly.

After a few more assurances that yes, she, a thirty-year-old woman who had lived on her own for nearly a decade, would be fine on her first trip out of state alone, she handed her mom the keys to her apartment, which was paid up until the end of the month. She backed toward her RV, waving. She knew that if she didn't get going now, she'd end up getting sucked into another round of goodbyes, and she was itching to hit the road.

Behind the wheel, she took a moment to look the still-unfamiliar dashboard over. Everything was digital, from the fuel gauge to the speedometer. It made her feel old; her own car still had analogue dials, and this RV was the first vehicle she'd driven with a backup camera. And the backup camera wasn't the only one. This thing had cameras all over the exterior, which was good since she was still getting used to driving what was essentially a mobile apartment.

"Well, here we go." She pushed the button to start the RV, and the diesel engine rumbled to life. Before putting it into drive, she glanced over at Cicero, who was in a cage strapped securely to the passenger seat. She wasn't truly alone, not with him. He was looking out the window, already keen to get going; he loved car rides, and she suspected it was because the speed and the sight of the landscape racing past reminded him of flying.

After typing her first destination into the built-in GPS, she looked out the window and waved goodbye to her parents one last time, then slowly pulled away from the curb, heading north.

For a woman born and raised in Michigan, the embarrassing truth was she had only been to the Upper Peninsula once, and she had been in fifth grade at the time. The only thing she really remembered from that trip was passing over the Mackinac Bridge. Hours after she left her parents' house, the greatest landmark in Michigan loomed in front of her. She paid her toll, turned down the radio, and eased the RV forward, glad that it wasn't a windy day. She'd heard of trucks being blown over in gales as they tried to cross the bridge.

There was a lot of traffic, but it still didn't take long to reach the bridge proper. The strange metal road made her tires hum, and she kept her speed slow as she stole glances across the expanse of water. It was easy to forget how big the Great Lakes were, but viewing Lake Michigan on one side and Lake Huron on the other, she was struck once again by their sheer immensity. She felt a surge of love for her state, but it didn't lessen her excitement over seeing the rest of the country in the slightest. Cicero let out a two-tone whistle, and she wondered if he was admiring the view too.

The UP had a different feel from the rest of the state, something that was noticeable from the moment they began descending off the bridge. Maybe she would feel differently if she lived up here, but it had been drilled into her all her life that people went up north to vacation. Something about crossing the bridge made her feel like her trip was just beginning, even though she'd already been driving for hours. With hours left until she reached Marquette, the small college city on Lake Superior's shore, she rolled the windows partway down and turned the radio back up, bobbing along to the music with her parrot.

By the time she started seeing signs for Marquette, it was well into the evening, and she was hungry. She'd stopped for fast food once, but she didn't want to get into the habit of doing that. The whole point of this trip was to explore, to try new things, and she wouldn't get the whole experience if she grabbed fast food burgers every time her stomach growled.

As she drove, she kept her eyes peeled for local restaurants. The sight of a slightly peeling sign promising the best pasties in the state seemed promising, and she took the next turn. She was still a mile or two outside of Marquette and was driving through forest dotted with the occasional house or roadside business. The restaurant wasn't too difficult to find, thanks to a handful of faded signs pointing the way. Called *Beth's Diner*, it didn't look like much. It was small, the paint as faded as the signs, with a few cars parked in the gravel lot. There was a slightly run-down house behind it and a stack of firewood for sale next to the door.

She hit her blinker and pulled into the lot, parking the RV along the grass median between the lot and the road, where she hoped it wouldn't be in anyone's way. Leaving the air-conditioning running for Cicero, she grabbed her purse, opened the driver's door, and stretched her legs out for the first time in hours.

"That's part one of the trip, done," she said, wiggling her toes in her sandals and making a mental note to stop to stretch more. As she inhaled the fresh, pine-scented air and listened to the drone of summer insects, she wondered if she could really do this. She was still in the same state, and she already felt so far from home.

Then she glanced back into the RV through the open driver's door and spotted Cicero, who was preening himself happily in the last of the day's sunlight and remembered that she had a king-size bed waiting for her tonight, along with her laptop, her movies, and all her favorite books. She was *driving* her home. It would take some getting used to, but she was sure it wouldn't be long until her RV was as much of a comfort zone as her apartment had been.

"I'll be right back, buddy," she told Cicero. "We'll eat dinner before driving the rest of the way to the campground. This is an adventure, isn't it?"

The bird ignored her in favor of straightening his bright red tail feathers. She smiled, shut the driver's door, and turned toward the diner. It was time to try the local cuisine.

CHAPTER THREE

"Can I get one of your original pasties and a chocolate milkshake?" Tulia asked. The interior of the diner was dated, but cozy, and the small menu offered a variety of pasties and ice cream desserts. Something else on the menu caught her eye. "Oh, and one of your breakfast pasties, please? Do you have hot sauce packets?"

It sounded better than the cereal she had in her RV, and she could heat it up in the microwave in the morning. She'd never had a pasty before, but from the description, it would be hard not to like them. The originals were a pastry crust filled with ground beef, onion, potatoes, carrots, and rutabaga. The breakfast pasties had scrambled eggs, cheese, potatoes, and bacon. Big enough to be an entire meal and able to be held while eaten, she could hardly get her hands on one. They were one of the many things she associated firmly with "Up North," and in her mind, the ultimate sign that she was really, finally, on the road trip of a lifetime.

The young woman behind the counter, who looked like she was in her mid-twenties, nodded and rang up the order. "Do you want one of those to go?"

"Both of them, actually." She was going to eat in her RV with Cicero. She wouldn't every time she stopped at a restaurant, but this whole trip was still new to him, and she wanted him to feel as comfortable as possible.

"I can get your original pasty and your milkshake out right away, but the breakfast one will be about ten or fifteen minutes. Is that okay?"

"That's fine, I'll just pop back in and get it in a few minutes."

The other woman beamed. "Great! It's worth the wait; I know there's probably about a hundred places that claim they have the best pasties in the state, but we really do."

Laughing and thanking the young woman, Tulia paid for her meal. Taking her milkshake and the bag containing her original pasty, she left the diner to rejoin Cicero. He whistled in greeting when she climbed into the RV. Easing past his cage where it was buckled into the passenger seat, she set her dinner on the small table her RV had come with and took Cicero's portable stand out of the tiny broom closet next to the RV's fridge. It was a perch screwed into a tripod, with a removable metal dish on one end.

She returned to the front to take Cicero out of his cage. He stepped up onto her fingers, his scaley feet cool on her skin. She put him on his perch before taking his plastic bin of food out of one of the latching cupboards and placing a small scoop into his bowl. After washing her hands with a shot of hand sanitizer she kept around for just that purpose, she sat down at the table and unwrapped her pasty. It was golden brown and smelled delicious. She broke off a bit of the crust to drop into Cicero's bowl, then picked up the plastic fork and knife the diner had provided with her order and dug in.

The pasty was every bit as good as she had hoped, and she didn't even manage to finish the whole thing. After sucking the last of the chocolate milkshake through the straw, she rewrapped the food and put it in the fridge, then tossed the bag and the rest of the trash in the garbage. With her stomach full, the sun starting to go down, and the pleasant feeling of being out from behind the driver's wheel after a long day, she was beat. Fighting back a yawn, she staggered the few steps to the RV's couch and sat down, bringing up the campground's information on her phone. She'd reserved an RV spot for the night, and knew the campground was somewhere just outside of Marquette, so it shouldn't be too far away. Tomorrow, she could take her car into town and do some sightseeing.

With a jolt, she remembered the breakfast pasty she had ordered. If it was the same size as the original pasty had been, she had a feeling pasties would be all she ate tomorrow—which wasn't necessarily a bad thing. Leaving her phone on the couch cushion, Cicero on his perch, and her purse on the dashboard —she had already paid, after all—she slipped out of the RV and made her way across the parking lot to the diner's entrance. Something rattled the dumpster around the corner of the building, and she quickened her step. It was probably just a raccoon, but it was a good reminder that even though she was still in Michigan, this area was wilder than what she was used to. Seeing a black bear was a real possibility up here. All of a sudden, she was very glad she would be sleeping in her RV and not in a flimsy tent.

Letting herself into the restaurant, she went up to the counter, where the same woman looked like she was clocking out. There was a full garbage bag on the ground next to her, and she had taken her apron off. Still, she had a smile waiting for Tulia and gestured to the paper bag on the counter.

"I was wondering if you'd forgotten. I added some hot sauce packets, so you should be all set."

"Thanks," Tulia said, grabbing the bag. She was all set to turn around and leave, but hesitated. This was the beginning of what was going to be a long trip. She was planning to be gone for months, and she didn't want to go that entire time without having a real, face-to-face conversation with another human being. Chatting on the phone or over a video call to her friends and her parents just wouldn't be the same. She was far from shy, but she'd never been the sort of person to go and strike up easy friendships with strangers either. Maybe now was the time to start?

She might as well go all-in on this new leaf she was turning over. She had more freedom than most people did to decide who she wanted to be now, and she didn't want to waste this fresh start to her life.

"My name is Tulia," she said, just a bit awkwardly. "I'm from Midland. I've never been up here before. Well, not since I was a kid. Have you always lived in the UP?"

"Born and raised," the woman said with a laugh.

She clicked a button on the computer, and it shut off. "My grandparents live in the Lower Peninsula, though, so I've been down there a lot. My name's Angela, by the way. Where all are you planning to visit while you're up here?"

"I'm not really sure," Tulia admitted. She followed Angela as the other woman grabbed the garbage bag and headed for the door. "I'm staying at a campground tonight, then I thought I'd drive around Marquette and maybe go to the beach tomorrow."

"If you have the time, you should definitely go to Pictured Rocks and Lake of the Clouds. They're both worth seeing, and there are good campsites near each of them. Oh, thanks."

Tulia held the door for her, then stepped out behind her. Angela set the garbage bag down and took out a ring of keys to lock the diner's door. "I'm not on a tight schedule or anything, so I'll look them up. Thanks for the suggestions."

"No problem." Angela hefted the garbage bag again and led the way around the corner toward the dumpster. "You should probably make reservations if you want to camp near a popular site, though. Summer's pretty busy up here. Of course, if you feel up to it, you can always camp at a state forest for—"

She broke off midsentence, and Tulia followed

her gaze to a dark puddle of liquid beside the dumpster. It looked almost black in the waning light.

"Something must have leaked out of the trash," Angela said uncertainly. "Can you get the lid? It's a pain to do when I've got a garbage bag in my other hand."

"Sure."

Tulia hefted one of the large lids up and glanced inside. A pair of blank eyes stared up at her, and she let the lid fall shut with a bang that disturbed a cloud of flies as she took a step back, barely missing the puddle of liquid with her shoe. It wasn't black; she could see that now. It was red. Blood red. She felt sick, and she swallowed rapidly to keep from vomiting.

"Hey, that almost fell on my arm. What happened?" Angela reached for the dumpster's lid.

"No, don't," she said, but it was too late. Angela opened the lid and looked inside, then stumbled back, screaming.

Tulia felt frozen, revulsion and horror mixing with a morbid curiosity. Some part of her was certain that she had somehow misunderstood her first glance into the dumpster. There couldn't be a man's body in there, his T-shirt stained with blood and one knee of his jeans ripped. It simply didn't fit with what she understood of the world. Stuff like this *didn't happen*. Not to her, at least. Not outside of movies and TV shows.

But she remembered his eyes, pale blue, blood-shot, and horribly blank. A fly had been crawling on one, before she disturbed it.

Suddenly certain she was going to puke, she staggered back around the corner of the building, but the sound of a diesel engine grumbling to life was enough to distract her from her nausea. She looked up just in time to see her RV pulling away.

Without her in it.

CHAPTER FOUR

"Wait, come back!"

She ran after the RV even though she knew it was pointless. It turned onto the road, the engine roaring as whoever was driving it put the gas pedal to the floor. As it began to pull away, Tulia slowed to a jog, then to a slow walk, still staring after it in disbelief. *Everything* was in there. Her phone, her purse … Cicero.

Fear for her feathered friend struck her like a knife in her gut, and she clapped her hands to her mouth, torn between screaming and crying. Why had she left her keys in the RV? Why hadn't she locked it behind her when she went back to get her breakfast pasty—which she had dropped somewhere between the dumpster and here.

The thought of what she and Angela had found in the dumpster brought her back to earth, but only slightly. Her worry for Cicero overwhelmed even the horror of seeing a dead body. He wasn't even in his cage! He might be a larger size for a bird, but compared to a human, he was so small and delicate. Would whoever had stolen her RV—and him along with it—be kind to him? Would they be gentle? Would they—

A wolf whistle made her jerk her head up. She looked around, searching for the source of the familiar sound. A high-pitched whistle, like a tea kettle, followed it, and finally, near the top of a tall tree, she spotted Cicero's grey form, his bright red tail standing out like a flag.

Relief washed through her, though it was tempered by the sight of just how *high* he was. Whoever had stolen the RV must have tossed him out, not wanting to deal with bird-napping on top of grand theft auto. Either that, or he had flown out in a panic when a stranger opened the door. Regardless of *how* he had gotten out, she was just glad he was safe.

"Cicero! Come here, buddy!" She held out her arm and, when he ignored her, she whistled for good measure.

He let out a whistle in response but didn't look

like he was planning on coming down from the tree any time soon. He *could* fly, and she'd trained him to fly to her for a treat indoors, but he'd never flown outside before, and he'd certainly never descended so far from so high up. She craned her neck, staring at him as she tried to work out what to do. The fire department might be willing to help, but chances were, their tall ladder and big truck would scare him. The last thing she wanted was for him to take off and disappear into the forest.

"Hey! Hey, um … Julia, right?"

She turned, leaving Cicero to his own devices in the tree for a moment as the reminder of the *other* disaster she was in the middle of came hurrying across the parking lot in the form of Angela with her phone pressed to her ear.

"Tulia," Tulia said, pronouncing it carefully. "Did you call the police?"

Angela nodded. "They're sending someone out here. I told them someone stole your RV too. Did you see what they looked like? Did you have anyone else in the RV with you? They're going to put an APB out."

Tulia realized, somewhat belatedly, that whoever had stolen her RV was probably the same person who had put the body in the dumpster. It might be a coincidence, but the chances that they were the same person was high.

Swallowing heavily, she shook her head. "I didn't see them, and it's just me."

Angela related her words to the dispatcher, and Tulia waited while the person on the other line talked for a little while longer. Finally, Angela put the phone in her pocket.

"They said we should wait inside and lock the doors until the police get here," she said. "But wait, I have to ask … um, did you do it?" At Tulia's blank look, she clarified. "Did you have anything to do with the guy in the dumpster?"

Her eyes widened. "No! Of course I didn't. I don't think I could have even lifted him in there without help. And why would I murder some stranger for no reason?"

"I had to ask," Angela said apologetically. "You're the only one who's come to the diner in the past two hours, and for all I know you're a serial killer or something." She took a deep breath. "I knew him. His name's Tom Platt. We used to be friends in high school, but he was a jerk, and I stopped seeing him a while ago. I heard he started selling drugs, and he got into a fight with my brother's friend once; I tried to avoid him after that. But he didn't deserve this."

"I'm sorry." She didn't know what else to say. As the two of them walked toward the diner's front entrance and Angela got the keys back out of her purse, Tulia looked at her out of the corner of her eye.

Had *she* had something to do with it? Angela seemed nice and all, but that didn't change the fact that Tulia had just met her. If that guy was a local, Angela might have some unpleasant history with him. Granted, she couldn't see the other woman hefting the man's body into the dumpster on her own, but maybe she was covering up for the *real* culprit.

Angela pushed the door open and half turned to gesture Tulia in, but before she could complete the movement, Tulia heard a flurry of wings, and Angela screamed and ducked.

She turned just in time to see Cicero flying at her like an ungainly feathered rocket. She raised her hand, hoping he would land on it, but he overshot her and alighted on the edge of the diner's roof. It was still beyond Tulia's reach, but it was much more accessible than the top of the tree.

"Good job, bud," she said, proud of him for braving the flight. "Look at you, you master of the skies."

"What is *that*?"

"His name is Cicero," she told Angela. "He's my bird."

Angela gave her a look that said she was very done with the day, but Tulia ignored it. She stretched an arm up toward Cicero, eyed the difference in height, then turned to her companion.

"You wouldn't happen to have a step ladder in the diner, would you?"

The diner *did* have a step ladder, and within minutes, Tulia had managed to convince a rather unhappy Cicero to step onto her hand. After looking him over to make sure he was unhurt, she shut him in the restroom with a bowl of water and some chopped up apple from the diner's fridge, just in time for the police to arrive on the scene.

What followed was the longest two hours of Tulia's life. Even though she knew for a fact that she was innocent of all things homicide related, talking to the authority about a murder gave her the worst case of nerves she'd ever had. They weren't even that interested in her as a suspect. Once they learned that the only helpful thing she could share was that she'd heard some rattling by the dumpster the first time she went into the diner, they switched over to asking her about her RV. Giving them the full list of everything she'd left in the RV had taken the longest, but she'd do whatever it took to help them track down the vehicle—and all her personal belongings—and with it, hopefully, the killer.

By the time they left, Tulia was exhausted. All she wanted was to go home—her *real* home, not the RV—and bury her head under some pillows. Instead, she was left facing the cold, hard reality of the fact that she had nothing, not even a cell phone to call her bank with. She'd just have to hope that whoever had stolen her RV didn't did too deeply into her personal belongings.

The diner had an old-fashioned pay phone in one corner, and she stared at it, pondering the irony of being a lottery winner without even a quarter to her name. The only number she had memorized was her parents' landline. She could call them, she knew. Doubtless, Angela could loan her some change from the till, and once she told her parents what had happened, they'd call a ride for her and get her a hotel room for the night before driving up here themselves in the morning. After getting back to Midland, she could go to the bank, cancel her cards, and start the long process of replacing what she had lost while she waited for the RV to turn up somewhere or the insurance to pay out on it.

Maybe that would be the responsible thing to do. She was still alive, unlike that man the coroner's office had taken away, and she had Cicero. She hadn't lost anything truly irreplaceable. She should go home and regroup and maybe find a good therapist to help with the trauma of the last few hours.

But the thing was … she knew if she did that, her trip was over. Oh, the police might recover the RV, or she could buy a new one, but if she went home now, after everything that had happened, she knew she would never do this again. And she wasn't ready to give up, not yet.

"Hey, I'm going to head home," Angela said, making her jump. Tulia turned away from the payphone to face her. "Do you need a ride somewhere?"

"If you don't mind, that would actually be really helpful."

Angela nodded and stared at Tulia for a moment, waiting for something. Finally, she said, "Okay, where do you need to go?"

"I…" Tulia opened her mouth, then closed it again, feeling helpless. Where *could* she go? She didn't have her wallet.

Angela seemed to come to that conclusion at the

same time she did. "Shoot, you don't have any money, do you?"

"I left *everything* in the RV," she admitted.

The other woman bit her lower lip, then sighed. "I hope I don't regret this, but you can stay at my place tonight if you want to. I've got an extra bedroom."

"Really? And Cicero … you wouldn't mind him?"

"I think there's an old rabbit cage in the shed. If you help me bring it in, he can stay in there. I don't know much about birds, but as long as he doesn't bite and he doesn't like, eat my couch or something, he's fine."

"Thank you so much," Tulia said. "I'll pay you back, I swear."

"Don't worry about it. Or if you insist, just stick around long enough tomorrow to help out here until the afternoon. The kid who was waiting tables for me in the mornings quit yesterday, and I haven't replaced him yet."

"I can do that," Tulia said, glad to be back on solid ground. "I'm a waitress."

"Really?" Angela shot a skeptical glance out the window, toward where the RV had been parked. The very expensive, very new RV.

"Well … it's a long story. But I was a waitress, up

until about six weeks ago. I know my way around a table."

The other woman laughed. It was strained, and she still looked exhausted after everything that had happened, but it was something. "I'll take your word for it, I guess. Go on and get your bird. I want to go home."

CHAPTER FIVE

Angela's house was two miles farther down the road, down a long dirt driveway through a scrubby forest that showed signs of recent logging. The house itself was a single story and had seen better days, but the inside was cozy, with houseplants on every windowsill and a half-finished afghan taking up two-thirds of the coffee table.

"Sorry for the mess," Angela said as she cleared her knitting away. "I wasn't expecting company. Well, my brother's supposed to come over today or tomorrow, but he doesn't count."

"It's a lovely house," Tulia said. "It's so private here. Are you renting, or do you own it?"

"This was my grandmother's house. She passed away last year. Technically, my mom owns it now, but she moved to Grand Rapids years ago and doesn't have any interest in moving back up here, so I've sort of inherited it. The diner was my grandmother's too. I helped her keep it running when she started having health issues, and now it's mine."

Tulia looked around with more interest, going over to the window to gaze up at the stars. The trees were barely visible through the darkness. It seemed so peaceful out here. She would have quite liked it if she wasn't worried sick about everything else.

"I'll go get that cage for your bird," Angela said, breaking into Tulia's thoughts. She gathered herself and went to help.

Before long, they had the old rabbit cage set up with a branch shoved through the bars as a makeshift perch. They placed some newspaper in the bottom as litter and added bowls for food and water. Cicero sat in the middle of the perch giving her the stink eye, but this was the best option Tulia could come up with for him. He was just lucky he hadn't been bird-napped along with the RV, though she knew he didn't understand that.

Angela opened up the guest room for Tulia, promising that it was clean, if maybe a bit dusty. It was fully dark by now, but even though she felt exhausted, she also felt far too wound up to sleep.

With any luck, the police would find her RV abandoned along the side of the road somewhere tomorrow, but luck hadn't exactly been with her this trip, so she wasn't holding out much hope.

Instead of locking herself in the guest room to stare at the ceiling and let her worries gnaw away at her, she sat with Angela out on the screened porch and chatted with the other woman while enjoying the summer night. Angela had been in this area all her life and had never traveled out of state, so she was interested in hearing about Tulia's travel plans—even if Tulia wasn't sure she was still going to go through with them.

"You're so lucky that you get to see the country," Angela said, sighing. "Even if I could afford a trip like that, I don't think I would be brave enough to go on my own. Do you mind if I follow you on your social media profile? I'd love to see pictures from the rest of your trip."

"You're welcome to add me, but I don't post on it much," Tulia admitted. "Maybe I *should* start posting about my trip, though. I'm sure some of my friends would like to hear about it."

"Ooh, you should start a blog." Angela looked eager as she warmed to her idea. "Travel blogs are pretty popular, aren't they? I bet a lot of people would be interested in reading it."

Tulia considered the suggestion. She did like to write; in fact, she'd considered starting a blog in the past, but at the time had figured her life was too boring for anyone to be interested in reading about it. Now, though, she might actually have some interesting stories to tell.

"If I get the RV back and keep going on my trip, I might do that," she said. "If the police don't find it soon, though, I think I'll probably just go home. I don't know if I have it in me to start the trip over from scratch."

"You should get back out there either way," Angela said. "If you can afford it, of course. Seriously, if you bought that RV with a waitressing job, tell me what restaurant you worked at. I'll sell the diner and move south in a heartbeat if there's a restaurant paying their staff enough to afford something like *that*."

Tulia shifted uncomfortably. She shouldn't have mentioned that she was—or had been—a waitress. It would have been better to let Angela assume she had some other random, high-paying job. It really *didn't* make sense for a waitress to be able to afford the sort of RV she was driving, but she didn't want to tell

Angela about the lottery. Not yet. Maybe not ever. She'd done a lot of research after she won, enough to know that people got *weird* around lottery winners.

"I'll see how I feel. Things always seem worse at night, anyway," she said, ignoring Angela's comment about the money. "I'll talk to the police tomorrow and see if—"

She broke off when Angela's phone rang, leaning back in her seat as the other woman shot her an apologetic glance and answered.

"Benny, what's up? I thought you were coming out here tonight. I already gave the guest room away, so if you're still coming out, you'll have to make do with the couch." She paused while whoever was on the other line spoke, then responded. "Ishpeming? I thought you were with a friend in Marquette." She sighed. "No, it's fine. I'll be there in about half an hour. Devon wants to come out too? Ugh, all right. I've got to get ready to go. Bye."

She ended the call and turned to Tulia, her expression apologetic. "That was my annoying little brother, who apparently needs a ride out here tonight. He's twenty and kind of bounces between my house and some of his friends' houses. I told him he could stay this week. I guess he and a friend of his are looking into getting jobs up here, so they're both going to crash here for a few nights."

"I'm so sorry. I'm completely in your way, aren't I? I could sleep on the couch tonight, or you could just drop me off at a motel."

"Don't worry about it; he was supposed to be here earlier this afternoon, so as far as I'm concerned, he lost his chance, and you've got dibs. The guest room is all yours. They can take the living room or camp outside; we've got tents, and it's nice out. They'll survive. I've got to run to Ishpeming to get them, and it will take me about an hour to get there and back again. Just like … don't burn the place down or rob me or whatever while I'm gone, 'kay?"

"If it would make you more comfortable, I can ride along with you." Tulia didn't think *she* would trust a stranger alone in her apartment so soon after meeting them, but Angela shook her head.

"You seem nice, and I don't really think you'll do anything. I just know my grandmother's probably rolling in her grave right about now. I'd better head out. Make yourself at home, and I promise we'll be quiet when we get back in case you're asleep."

Slightly overwhelmed at how quickly she seemed to have been wrapped up in Angela's life, she waited around awkwardly while Angela put her shoes on and grabbed her purse, then waved goodbye as she pulled down the driveway and vanished into the night.

Being alone in a stranger's house was an uncomfortable experience. She got ready for bed as quickly as possible, taking a fast shower and making sure to tidy up behind her, then joined Cicero in the guest room. It had been a long day for both of them. She sat up with him for a few minutes, talking softly and promising things would seem better in the morning, then she shut off the bedside lamp and lay down. The silence seemed louder than the traffic outside her apartment ever was, and she wasn't sure how long it took her to fall asleep.

She woke in the morning to the smell of bacon and pancakes, relieved that she hadn't been murdered during the night. She got up, made an effort to comb her hair out with her fingers, and straightened her rumpled clothes. Promising Cicero to bring him back some food, she wandered out of the bedroom and into the kitchen.

She was greeted with the sight of two unfamiliar men eating a feast of breakfast food at the kitchen table. One of them had to be Angela's brother; he had the same brown hair and Roman nose as she did. The other had short black hair and a tattoo along one arm.

Both of them stared at her when she came into the room.

"You're up! Sorry, did we wake you?" Angela's cheerful voice drew Tulia's eyes to the stove, where even more pancakes and bacon were in the process of being made. Her stomach rumbled at the sight.

"I think it was the smell of bacon that woke me up," she admitted. "And that's not something I'd ever complain about."

Angela laughed. "Go ahead and grab a plate. There's some orange juice in the fridge. You can join the others at the table if you want. Benny, introductions!"

Angela's brother straightened up, suddenly remembering his manners. "Sorry. I'm Benny, Angela's brother, and this is my friend Devon. You're the woman whose RV got stolen, right?"

Tulia nodded as she accepted a plate loaded with bacon and pancakes and maple syrup from Angela. "Yep. Angela's been very nice to let me stay here. I'll figure out a way to get out of your hair today."

"Not so fast," Angela said as she brought the orange juice over to the table. "You promised to help me at the diner, remember?"

Tulia could hardly go back on her word now after Angela had gone out of her way to be so kind to her, so she was quick to nod. "Of course. I'll stick around as long as you need me to."

"Good. Because the police might have left crime scene tape all over half the parking lot, but they didn't say anything about closing the diner, and my bills don't pay themselves. Hey, does your bird eat pancakes?" She tilted a plate to show Tulia a single, perfect pancake the size of a silver dollar—plain, without butter or syrup—and Tulia smiled. It wasn't necessarily as healthy as his parrot food, but it was something he could eat safely, and he was always thrilled to get human food.

"He'll love it."

She brought Cicero his breakfast, then returned to the chaos of the kitchen to finish her own food. She still didn't know what the future was going to bring, but things did look brighter in the morning light. She'd keep her word, help Angela, and then she would talk to the police and see if they had any inkling as to where her RV had gotten to. She wanted to see this trip through to the end.

CHAPTER SIX

The four of them carpooled to Beth's Diner together since Angela only had one car. Benny and Devon dropped them off, then left to head to Marquette, where they were supposedly going to look for jobs. Tulia had learned that the two of them had been best friends since elementary school, that Devon was an out-of-work welder, and that Benny had never pursued higher education. Though Angela was only five years older than her brother, she acted more like a mother to him than a sister.

She was curious as to *why* Angela's mother and father were out of the picture, but kept her mouth shut. Common sense told her that some things simply shouldn't be asked, especially not to someone she'd known less than twenty-four hours.

The crime scene tape was still up in the parking lot, marking off the dumpster and a good area around it, but Angela simply parked by the other side of the building and headed for the door, waving goodbye to her brother as Tulia hurried to catch up to her. She'd left Cicero at Angela's house while she worked since a restaurant really wasn't the place for a parrot, and she'd fashioned a few homemade toys for him to keep him entertained while she was gone.

Inside the diner, Angela ran through the opening routine with a speed that was daunting. She kept up a cheerful chatter all the while, and when she spotted Tulia standing awkwardly near a table, unsure what to do, she said, "There's a couple aprons in the kitchen, and the drawer next to them are full of name tags. We don't have Tulia, but feel free to pin one on and be someone else for the day if you want. We've got a lot of regulars, and they'll want a name to call you by."

Tulia found a mostly unstained apron and affixed a nametag that read *Kim* onto it, then scrounged a notepad and pen and poured over the menu, trying to memorize as much of it as she could. It wasn't a very big menu, thankfully; besides the breakfast pasty, the breakfast menu was pretty average. They didn't start serving lunch until eleven, though for all Tulia knew, she'd be there well into the afternoon.

She was reliant on Angela for a ride into Marquette if she wanted to go anywhere, and from the sound of it, the other woman spent most of her time at the diner.

The morning started out slow, but as time wore on, the little diner got moderately busy. As Angela had said, most of the customers seemed to be regulars, and they all had friendly questions for her. She didn't mention the missing RV or the body she and Angela had found but was happy to chat with people other than that. It was a lot more laid back than her last job had been, though the tips weren't nearly as good. At least she had some cash to her name again, though Angela insisted on giving her free food for lunch, so she didn't get to spend it.

Just before lunch, a shiny black SUV pulled into the diner's parking lot. Angela watched as two men got out. The shorter of the two was wearing black slacks; the taller had khaki ones, but they were both wearing nice button-up shirts and had matching sunglasses. They drew her eyes because they looked so out of place in this run-down diner, and her eyes weren't the only ones they drew as they came in.

The taller one, who had medium-length dark hair that was slicked back, spotted her and made a beeline for her. For a second, she wondered if he was a cop who wanted to talk about Tom, but he just said, "Can you get us a booth for two?"

"Of course. Right this way." She led them to a booth against the back wall and prepared to take their drink orders, but before she could, the man introduced himself. "Samuel Noble," he said, holding his hand out. She shook it bemusedly, wondering if he introduced himself to every waitress who served him. She'd met weirder people in her time in the service industry. "And this is Marc. We're from Ohio. Are you a local here?"

He didn't sound like he was from Ohio. If she had to guess, she'd put his accent somewhere along the northern part of the east coast. Still, if they were tourists, it explained a lot.

"Nope," she said, only belatedly realizing how odd that question was. She was working here. Shouldn't they assume she was a local?

"I see. Then I suppose I can't ask you to recommend your favorite dish on the menu."

She gave him a tight smile. She hated that question. Taste in food was such a personal thing, and she didn't want to feel like it was her fault if a customer tried what she recommended and didn't like it. Still, if they were tourists, they were probably after the same thing she had been.

"The original pasty is pretty good. It's the only one I've tried."

"I think we'll both get one," he said without consulting his companion, who looked vaguely irritated at the whole exchange. He handed the menu she had given him back to her, then hesitated. "Just one more thing. If you're not a local, how'd you end up serving tables here?"

"I ran into some transportation issues, and the owner was nice enough to let me stay with her last night and work it off today," she answered, taking the menu back. "Your order will be right out."

She felt a bit bad about her short response but was relieved to walk away and not be called back. Samuel asked strange questions, and after finding a man's body, she was a bit more on edge than normal.

Thankfully, they didn't ask her any more odd questions, though they did stay for quite a while, and she caught both Samuel's and Marc's eyes on her more than once. It was after noon when two other employees showed up. A woman in her forties made Tulia give up her *Kim* name tag, and an elderly man took over for Angela in the kitchen. Angela chatted with them both for a few minutes, shooting furtive looks toward the side of the building where the dumpster was and where the body had been found. Finally, she came to find Tulia, and the two of them went out to the parking lot together. To Tulia's surprise, Angela's car was waiting for them there.

The other woman laughed at the confusion she must have been wearing on her face as they got into the car. "Yeah, Benny dropped it off about half an hour ago and walked home. Do you want to head into town? I know you wanted to talk to the police about your RV, but I was thinking maybe we could do some touristy stuff too since you're missing out on all of that. Maybe go to the beach? Have you ever been to Lake Superior?"

"No. I know it's the deepest of the Great Lakes, but that's all. I've been to Lake Huron and Lake Michigan, though. I'd definitely like to see it."

"Sweet. I know a nice beach that's usually not too busy, even with all the tourists in summer. We can swing by—" She broke off to frown at the diner, where the woman who had taken Tulia's *Kim* name tag and pinned it to her own chest was waving at them with a phone in her hand. Angela opened the car door and undid her seatbelt. "I'd better go see what Kim wants."

Tulia watched as Angela hurried over to the woman whose name tag she had stolen and accepted the phone. A moment later, she turned to face the car and started waving frantically at Tulia. She scrambled to get out, her heart in her throat. Was it the police? Did they have more information?

She jogged the short distance to Angela, who had the phone pressed to her ear like she was afraid it would escape. "Yeah, I know where that is," she was saying. "We can be there in about twenty minutes. She's with me now. Great, thank you so much, officer. That's great news." She said a quick goodbye, hung up, and handed the phone back to Kim before turning to Tulia.

"What is it? What happened?"

"They found your RV! The officer I spoke to said it's in good condition, nothing seems to be damaged or anything. They tried calling my cell first, I guess, but called the diner when they couldn't get through. No one gets good service out here, not until you reach Marquette."

"Oh, my goodness." Tulia had to take a step back, feeling almost faint from relief. She'd *hoped* they'd find her RV but hadn't really thought it would happen this soon. Part of her had been certain that whoever had stolen it would have wrecked it somehow before abandoning it. "I can't believe it."

"It's parked along an access road near Ishpeming. I know roughly where it is. Are you ready to go?"

"Definitely." Tulia barely kept herself from sprinting back to the car. She wouldn't be able to truly relax until she saw the RV and verified for herself that it was in good shape. Angela hadn't said anything about her purse or other personal belongings, but if she had to, she could get all of that replaced, even though it would be a huge chore to do.

Having the RV back meant one very important thing to her. Her trip wasn't over yet.

CHAPTER SEVEN

Angela drove the twisting roads away from Marquette while Tulia looked out the window, eager and anxious in equal measure. She'd half convinced herself that she would never see the RV again, and part of her still couldn't believe this was real.

When the other woman pulled off onto a bumpy dirt road that either didn't have a road sign or had one that was so overgrown Tulia hadn't spotted it, she sat up straighter. It seemed crazy to her that someone had taken her RV out *here* and just left it. Where would they have gone? Had they just walked into the woods on foot?

She voiced the thought aloud, and Angela responded, saying, "Ishpeming is only a mile or two further down the main road. Whoever dumped your

RV here probably just walked to town. That RV would draw a lot more eyes than someone walking along the shoulder would."

"So, they stole it from the diner just to dump it twenty miles away?" Tulia asked, frustrated.

"Don't forget that whoever stole it probably *killed* Tom." Angela shot her a look. "It was an escape vehicle. I doubt they were ever going to take it to a chop shop, or whatever it is you're envisioning people usually do with stolen vehicles."

She frowned but had to admit that Angela was right. The RV had probably just been a convenient way for the killer to escape the scene of the crime. Now that she had the chance to think about it more, it did make sense that they would want to dump it as soon as possible. She'd nearly driven herself crazy imagining that the thief would be galivanting around the country in her RV, but in retrospect, that would have been a good way for them to get caught.

Angela rounded a corner, and suddenly, there it was. The RV had been pulled off slightly to the side of the road, but it wasn't for enough over to be in the ditch. Her car was still attached to the back, looking dusty but not any worse for wear other than that. There were two police vehicles, one parked in front of the RV and the other parked behind it, both with their lights flashing. Angela pulled off the road behind the first police vehicle, and as the two of them got out, an officer came over to greet them.

"Is one of you the owner of these vehicles?" he asked, gesturing at the RV and the car.

"I am," Tulia said, stepping forward. "I'm Tulia Blake."

"I'm Officer Willis. Can I see some ID, ma'am?"

She faltered since she didn't even have her purse, then brightened. "I don't have it on me, but if my purse is in there, then my driver's license will be inside."

She described her purse for him and waited with bated breath while he went to speak with a police officer who was in the RV. A moment later, he came out holding her purse in one hand and a rush of pure relief went through her. Somehow, miraculously, the thief hadn't taken her valuables with him when he dumped the RV.

After comparing her face to the picture on her ID, Officer Willis handed over her purse, then led the way to the front of the RV. "I'm sure you'll be relieved to hear that there doesn't appear to be any obvious damage to the vehicle or your belongings. Since the person who stole it is wanted for questioning for a homicide in addition to theft of a motor vehicle, we obtained a warrant to search the RV for evidence that could help us track them down. We're nearly done with that, but I'd like you to take a look through it as well and tell us if anything seems to be missing or out of place."

"Of course. Will I be able to get it back when you're done, or will you guys impound it or something?" She had no idea how this sort of thing worked.

"Depends on if we find anything," he replied with a shrug. "If it's clean, you'll be good to go. If we find forensic evidence, we may need to impound it. Like I said, though, we're nearly done, and we haven't found anything yet. Whoever stole this thing was either very careful or wasn't in it long enough to leave anything behind."

Tulia nodded, unable to take her eyes off the RV. She hadn't had it long, but already, it felt like she was greeting an old friend. She really, really hoped this nightmare would be over soon.

It was the sound of tires on gravel that made her finally tear her eyes away from the RV and look back down the road the way they'd come. A vaguely familiar SUV came around the corner with two men seated in the front, but she didn't fully place it until the driver slowed to a stop across from where she,

Angela, and Officer Willis were standing and rolled down his window.

"Samuel?"

"You know them?" Angela said in confusion.

"He was at the diner earlier today," she explained as Sam looked between them.

"Is everything all right?" he called out, his eyes focused on her even though he was talking to their entire group.

"We've got it handled, sir. You can move along," Officer Willis responded. His tone was brusque, but not unfriendly.

"I see." Sam gave Tulia another long look, then glanced at her RV. A furrow formed between his brows, but his expression was quick to clear. "I'm glad you found your RV. I hope the rest of your trip is enjoyable."

"Thanks," she said, a bit awkwardly. All three of them watched as Sam rolled his window up and continued down the road. She was staring after his car as it disappeared around a curve in the road when Officer Willis cleared his throat.

"A friend of yours?"

"Not at all," she said. "I met him at the diner earlier. He asked all sorts of weird questions. He seemed very nosy, but nice enough, I guess."

"I've never seen him before in my life," Angela said. "He's obviously a tourist, of course, with that accent. How did he know we were out here, though?"

"Do you know his full name?" Officer Willis asked.

"Samuel Noble," Tulia said. "He introduced himself, and we chatted a bit at the diner. He left hours ago, though. I have no idea how he knew we were on this road. The other one's name is Marc, but I didn't get his last name, and he didn't say much."

"I'll look into it," Officer Willis said, frowning. Tulia could guess what he was thinking. How suspicious was it that this guy none of them knew happened to drive past them down this little dirt road that led nowhere?

They didn't have time to talk about it further. The police officer who had been looking through the RV came out, and Officer Willis gave Tulia the all clear to reclaim her vehicle. He wished her luck, and she promised to report it if she later discovered that anything was missing. Then, the police left, and she and Angela were alone on the quiet road with no sound but the drone of insects around them.

"Thanks for the ride out here," Tulia said, leaning against the side of the RV. "I'll stop by your house and get Cicero, if that's okay, then I can get out of your hair."

"Are you going to head out already?" Angela asked, sounding disappointed. "You haven't even gone to the lake yet."

"I haven't really decided yet," Tulia admitted. "I had a campground reservation for three nights, but I didn't show up yesterday, and they might have cancelled it. I do still want to explore the area, though."

"Why don't you just park your RV at my place?" Angela suggested. "I don't have hookups for it, but it would probably be a lot quieter than a campground, and I can show you around Marquette if you feel up to it this evening."

"Really? I don't want to intrude..."

"I mean it," Angela said firmly. "You are more than welcome to stay."

Tulia bit her lip. "Yeah, all right. I'll camp out on your property for at least tonight. As long as your brother doesn't mind."

Angela shrugged. "It's not his house. Besides, he and Devon are good guys. I know, maybe we can do a cookout tonight. We can pick up some food when we go into town."

Tulia laughed. "All right, that does sound fun. But

I'm buying, no arguments." She already felt in debt to Angela, and now that she had her purse back, she could begin paying the other woman back for her kindness.

They said goodbye and promised to meet up again at Angela's house. Tulia climbed into the RV with a light heart. She'd gotten all of her possessions back and could finally move on and start enjoying her trip. As she started the engine and carefully pulled onto the road, she hit the button to turn the radio on and hummed along to the song that played. She had almost completely forgotten that the person who had killed Tom was still out there somewhere.

CHAPTER EIGHT

They stopped off at Angela's house to move Cicero over from the converted rabbit cage to his own cage and give him some actual parrot food instead of questionably healthy human food. She set her laptop up to play music for him while they were gone, then plugged in her cell phone, which had died sometime between yesterday and now. Next, she sent a text message to her very concerned parents, promising them she was okay and would call them later. Then she went outside in time to see Angela toss Benny, who was sitting on the porch, her car keys.

"Where'd Devon go?" she asked after he caught them.

"He took a walk out in the woods," Benny said. "You know how he gets."

"Did you guys argue or something?" Angela asked, raising an eyebrow. Her brother just shrugged, and she sighed. "Right, well, Tulia and I are going into town. We're going to pick some stuff up for a bonfire this evening, so if you don't have anything pressing to do, maybe you could stack some wood for us. How'd your job hunt go?"

He shrugged again, and Angela grumbled all the way to Tulia's car, which they unhooked from the back of the RV together. "You'd think he was still fourteen with the way he acts. He's twenty, and he's never held a job longer than a few months! He drives me absolutely insane."

Tulia kept her mouth shut, not sure what to say. She didn't have any siblings and didn't feel qualified to give advice, not that she had any.

"I love him, of course," Angela continued as she got into the passenger seat next to Tulia. "I mean, he's my little bro. I'd do anything for him. I want him to do better for his own good, you know?"

"I'm sure he'll come around eventually," Tulia said. She backed up and turned around, then glanced over at the other woman. "Where are we going?"

"That's up to you. You're the tourist. What do you want to see?"

"I kinda wanted to swing by the Northern Michigan University campus, just to see it. My dad almost went there when he went to college. And of course, I'd like to go to Lake Superior, and I'd like to see Marquette's downtown district. Other than that … I'm happy to do anything."

Angela grinned. "I've never played tour guide before, but I think I'm going to be good at it. Turn left on the road; we'll be in town in no time."

Two hours later, Tulia was feeling every inch the tourist. They'd swung through the college campus, which wasn't very busy since it was summer. It turned out Angela had done a semester of school there, and she explained that the campus had underground tunnels for when the weather was especially bad in winter. Tulia thought that was an extremely neat feature, though it made her wonder just how bad winter could get up here.

Their next stop was the downtown part of Marquette, where they parked along the curb and got out to walk the hilly streets. Unlike the campus, Marquette was swarming with people, both tourists and locals taking advantage of the nice weather to get some fresh air and do some shopping. Tulia was resigned to window shopping until she remembered that she could actually *afford* to do more than look now, and she bought herself a Marquette sweatshirt that had a stylized rendition of the city on it. She also purchased a handmade scarf with autumn colors that she loved, even if she wouldn't need to wear it for months yet. She bought Angela a scarf of her own when she spotted the other woman eyeing one and forced the other woman to accept the gift by claiming she still owed her for all of the help she had been giving her.

Finally, they got back into the car and headed toward the beach. Angela directed her away from the busier spots right by the city, and they drove along the coast for a few miles until Angela had her turn down an unmarked dirt road. She was skeptical, but after driving only a few hundred feet, the road turned sharply and ended at a pebbly beach lined with trees. The lake stretched in front of them, endless and blue.

Tulia felt a thrill as she stepped out of the car and the lakeside breeze tugged at her hair. *This* was what she had wanted to experience on her trip. New things, things that reminded her of the expanse and beauty of her country.

"It's gorgeous," she said as Angela joined her. "This is an amazing spot."

"Isn't it? You'll get a few people here sometimes, but it's too rocky for swimming, and there's no boat launch, so even the locals don't use it much. You can wade in, though the water's going to be chilly."

"I can brave a little chill."

They walked down the beach together. Once they reached the edge of the waves that lapped at the shore, Tulia slipped her sandals off and went forward until the cold water splashed over her feet. She smiled as she gazed out across the lake, the far shore lost to the horizon. It was amazing to think of the sheer *size* of Lake Superior, and she wondered what secrets might hide in its depths. She could now say she had visited three of the five Great Lakes. Hopefully, by the end of her trip, she would have seen many more natural landmarks. This was just the beginning.

"You know, my grandmother had a boat that she left me," Angela said from behind her. She hadn't waded in and was instead searching along the beach for interesting rocks. "I don't take it out much, but if you're still going to be around this weekend, we can go out on the lake."

"I wouldn't—"

"Stop it, you wouldn't be imposing. Do you have any idea how boring my life is? Most of my friends moved away after high school. The few who stuck around either left after college, or they stuck around but have jobs and families. I spend like ninety percent of my time either working or thinking about working, and the rest of the time, I'm wondering when my brother will get his life together. Do you really think I'm anything but happy to have an excuse to go have fun this weekend?"

"All right, all right," Tulia said with a laugh. "I can stay another day or two. I do want to go out on the lake. I've only ever been kayaking, and I've never been on a real boat."

It was something to look forward to. She didn't want to stay *too* much longer, though. She had a lot to see, and she'd never complete her road trip if she got sidetracked so easily.

They returned to Angela's house that evening as it was getting dark out. Benny and Devon had already started a fire in the ring of stones in Angela's yard, and Tulia made sure Cicero could see them out the RV's window from his cage. Parrots couldn't safely be around smoke, or she would have tried to put his harness on so he could join them. As it was, she made frequent trips back to the RV to bring him treats—bits of broken off graham cracker, some watermelon and grapes they'd bought at the store, and a chopped off piece of corn on the cob, which would keep him occupied for most of the evening.

She and Angela chatted during the cookout, and eventually Devon joined in on the discussion, giving his opinion of a movie they'd all seen when it had been released the year before. Benny remained quiet, shooting his friend glances that made Tulia wonder what their argument earlier had been about. Benny looked almost … scared.

She glanced over at Devon as he said, "I don't know which one of you bought all this food, but it's all great. My girlfriend and I had a campfire last week, but we didn't think to cook anything but hot dogs on sticks. These brats are way better."

"That was Tulia," Angela said. "She insists that she still owes me for letting her crash in the guest room, even though I made her work all day at the diner."

"Well, I owe you one," Devon said, smiling as he raised his can of pop in a toast. She smiled back at him, then glanced over at Benny, who was scowling at his friend.

Whatever their argument had been over, she had a feeling it was more serious than Angela, who was currently lighting marshmallows on fire before blowing them out and eating them whole, seemed to think. At the end of the day, though, it wasn't her business or her problem. She did her best to put all of it—Tom's murder, the RV theft, whatever was going on with Angela's brother and his best friend, and all her other worries—out of her mind and enjoy the evening.

CHAPTER NINE

It was past midnight when Tulia finally retreated to her RV for the night. It was her first night sleeping in it, but she was too tired to really enjoy the sensation of being securely snuggled into her own home on wheels. After taking a quick shower, mindful of how limited her water supply was with no hookups, she tucked herself in to the generously sized bed and barely had time to remember that she hadn't called her parents like she had promised before she was out like a light.

When she woke up, it wasn't to the sun's cheerful morning light, but rather the soft red flicker of the dying campfire through the RV's blinds. Bleary-eyed, she sat up in bed and looked around. She could only have been out for a few hours at most, but what had woken her? The RV was quiet, and a quick check of her phone showed no new notifications.

She got out of bed and walked over to the window, lifting the blinds up to peek out. The fire was almost out—it was a pit of embers with only a few flickering flames. When she had gone to bed, the others had still been up, watching it, but now she didn't see anyone. Would Angela really have gone to bed with an unattended fire outside? She liked to think she wouldn't, but the truth was, she barely knew the woman.

"At least I didn't wake up to my RV burning down around me," she muttered. That would have been just her luck, considering how the trip had gone so far.

She shuddered a bit at the memory of finding the body and tried to push the images away. Whoever had killed that poor man would be caught, and it didn't have anything to do with her. By this time next week, she would be long gone. While she felt terrible for him, she was just a waitress—not even that now. She knew there wasn't anything she could do to help, so why drive herself crazy thinking about it?

She stared at the dying fire for another moment, trying to decide whether or not she should go out there and kick dirt over it or something. It didn't *look* like it was in danger of spreading, but she was sure that was what most people thought hours before a forest burned down around them.

Something thudded against the opposite side of the RV, making her jump and making the entire vehicle shake. Cicero shifted in his cage, having joined her in wakefulness.

"What the heck?" she whispered as she crept toward a window on the other side. "Was that a bear or something?"

The last time she'd thought a mysterious noise might be a bear, it had turned out to be someone stashing a dead body in a dumpster. This time she almost hoped it *was* a bear.

Before she reached the window, though, she heard voices. Inching closer, she peeked out the window and saw two people standing against the side of her RV, their forms shadowy in the dark. She couldn't tell who they were and couldn't make out what they were saying. Curious, she fumbled at the window, trying to remember how to open it. Finally, she found the latch and managed to inch the window open silently.

"… know something is going on. Why are the two of you acting so strange?"

It was Angela's voice, low and intense. A man

responded. She didn't know Benny and Devon enough to be sure which it was.

"You can't guess?" He scoffed. "The police are going to figure it out eventually. We're all going to be caught up in it when they do. Why are you pretending nothing happened? You've spent the past few days prancing around with your new friend, when you should have been spending them getting ready for the fallout."

"I don't know what you're talking about," Angela hissed.

"I don't believe you," the man hissed right back. "And the police won't either. A man *died*. That doesn't just go away."

"Stop it. Just leave me alone." Her voice cracked, and the man withdrew.

"Pretending it didn't happen won't make it go away," he said in a parting remark before he walked around the RV, leaving Angela to sag against the side of the vehicle in the dark. Tulia wondered if she should say something, reveal herself and make sure Angela was okay, but before she could decide, the other woman straightened up and took a deep breath, then went the same way the man had gone around the RV.

Tulia went back over to the other window and

looked out. The man wasn't visible. He had probably already gone into the house, but Angela took the time to kick some sandy soil over the fire and pick up some of the trash that had been left out before going in. She didn't look at the RV once, and Tulia watched her until the door closed behind her.

Then, she retreated to her bed and lay on top of the covers, staring up at the ceiling as she wondered what she had just overheard. She'd been trying hard not to dwell on finding Tom's body. It felt over-whelming, monumental, and like something she just couldn't deal with. She'd thought that, once she had the RV back, she was done with her involvement in things.

But by the sound of it, whoever had been talking to Angela knew something about what had happened … and thought Angela knew about it too.

The thought raised goosebumps on her arms. She'd believed Angela was exactly what she acted like: an average, friendly young woman with a good heart and the kindness to offer her home to a stranger in need. Had she somehow been hiding knowledge about Tom's killer all along? Was she involved?

She turned over onto her side, laying her head on her pillow and staring blankly at the wall beside her. She didn't want to tell Angela what she had overheard, but she knew she couldn't keep it a secret. It would eat at her, and if what she'd heard could help the police solve a murder, wasn't it her responsibility to share it?

Uncomfortable, worried, and wishing she'd slept through the night without hearing a thing, she closed her eyes and tried to sleep, telling herself that things would look better in the morning. They always did.

She woke up bleary-eyed and still tired. It was strange to go through her morning routine in such a cramped space, and her favorite sweatshirt, which she had put on when it started getting chilly last night, smelled like campfire smoke. It was a reminder that she'd have to do laundry at laundromats for the duration of her trip; her RV may be fancy, but it didn't exactly have a washing machine.

The inconveniences were small, but it was a reminder that she still had a lot to get used to. This new lifestyle of hers wasn't permanent, but it *would* last a few months, at least, unless she chickened out and went home early. She knew that, within a few weeks, she would probably have figured out all the little tips and tricks to make life on the road easier, but that time felt like a long way off just then.

Once she got dressed and gave Cicero his breakfast and a kiss on the beak, she stepped outside to find

Angela waiting for her on the porch. The other woman had a smile on her face, but it looked strained, and Tulia didn't know if it was in her head or if something had changed in the other woman since last night.

"Good morning! I'm about to head to the diner. Don't feel like you have to, but I was wondering if you wanted to come with me? I totally understand if you'd rather do tourist stuff."

Tulia had been thinking she might find somewhere to go hiking; Cicero could go with her on his harness, and it would give both of them a chance to get some fresh air. But now, with what she'd overheard last night fresh on her mind, she knew she couldn't waste this opportunity to try to figure out exactly what it was that Angela knew.

"I don't mind helping out at the diner," she said. "I'm ready to leave whenever you are."

Before long, she found herself slipping back into her old habits of being a waitress for the second time in as many days. The diner was a bit busier than it had been the day before, probably because it was a Friday and people had the excuse of celebrating the weekend early. Still, it was easy enough to keep up with her tables, and she even managed to take the time to chat with a few of the guests who wanted to know her name and her story. Whenever she went to the kitchen to pick up an order, she took the chance to chat with Angela—just a few sentences here and there, keeping up an intermittent stream of conversation between them. She waited for a good opportunity to ask about the murder, or even to ask more about Tom in case it gave her insight into why he might have been killed.

But then two all too familiar men walked through the door, and she found herself face to face with Samuel and Marc again. Only this time, she wasn't sure she believed they were just friendly tourists. She still had no idea how they'd come across her and Angela when they went to fetch her RV the day before, and she didn't like it.

"Table for two, please," Sam said, giving her his crooked smile as he slid his sunglasses to the top of his head.

"Right this way." She kept her voice brusque and professional as she led them to a booth—far from the other guests. She wasn't sure what their deal was, but something about them struck her as different from everyone else here.

"Thank you," Sam said, taking a seat. His silent partner sat across from him and nodded at her. She passed them their menus.

"What can I get you to drink?"

"Just water for me, miss," Sam said. "I'm surprised to see you here again. Didn't you say you were just helping out for the day?"

"I decided to stick around a bit longer," she replied, giving him her much-practiced customer service smile. "Speaking of surprises, how did you know where we were yesterday?"

He raised an eyebrow, seeming taken aback that she'd brought it up. "It was just happenstance on our part. There was supposed to be a small lake back there, according to our GPS. Turns out, the access to it was overgrown years ago, but at the time we were just hoping to get some fishing in."

"Right." She looked the two of them up and down, then glanced out the window toward their shiny black SUV. With their neatly pressed button up shirts and matching sunglasses, they looked more like special agents than fishermen, but she wasn't going to call them out on it.

"I'll have a diet soda," the other man said, cutting into the drawn-out silence.

She nodded and, without another word, spun on her heel to get their drinks. When she came back to take their orders, they put their requests in without hassle, but Sam drew her into conversation again when she came back with their meals.

"So, where are you heading next?"

The question seemed like a non sequitur and caught her by surprise. "Hmm?"

"You mentioned you were on a road trip, and last I saw you, you had a fancy RV you'd just recovered. That must have been lucky, having it found so quickly."

"I'm heading to Wisconsin," she said shortly. She didn't want to be too specific, and almost immediately wished she hadn't even said that.

He exchanged a glance with his companion. "I see. And that will be stop number … what, in your little trip?"

Irritated with the way he was speaking to her, almost like he was interrogating her, she snapped, "It's none of your business. I'm sorry, but I'm trying to work. If you need anything else, let me know, but I have other guests to attend to."

She didn't wait for a response before she walked away. Maybe he was just another creep who didn't know when his attention wasn't wanted—she'd met far too many of them in her time as a waitress—but something about the two men seemed off in a way that she didn't have experience with. It was like they knew something she didn't, something they were holding over her head.

But she'd never seen them before this trip.

She kept her distance from them as best she could, hoping they would eat and leave quickly, but they nursed their coffees and stayed all the way up to when Kim and the older man came in to replace her and Angela. They left as Angela was counting out her tips, and she watched them drive away in their SUV, hoping that would be the last she saw of them.

She realized, as she and Angela walked out to her car, she'd been so distracted by the two of them that she had completely forgotten to try to figure out what Angela knew about the murder.

CHAPTER TEN

That evening, she sat at the small table in her RV while Cicero wandered the floor, looking for trouble. Angela had offered to do another campfire or for her to come in and watch a movie with her, Benny, and Devon, but Tulia had declined. Benny and Devon still weren't talking, the former sullen and quiet, and the latter almost forcibly chatty as if he needed to cover up the oppressive silence. Angela seemed short tempered with both of them but kept a smile on her face for Tulia's sake.

All in all, it wasn't the sort of atmosphere she wanted to spend extra time embroiled in. She was beginning to regret promising to stay for the boating trip and just hoped the coming of the weekend cheered everyone up.

She had so much on her mind and no one to tell it to. Even though she had finally called her parents and reassured them that she was alive, just busy, she hadn't told them what had happened. They would just worry and insist she come home. She didn't want to make things worse for them. She *could* tell one of her friends, she supposed, but Luis was a part of their friend group, and she didn't want her trip to get back to him yet. She knew a lot of stuff was going to hit the fan when he finally figured out that she'd come into serious money, and she wanted to have at least a couple states in between them before that happened. So, while her friends knew she was taking a road trip "to find herself," as far as they were concerned, she was just puttering along in her little car and scraping the bottom of her bank account to do it.

What it all boiled down to was that she had no one to turn to with everything that had happened. Well, she could talk to Cicero, and he might even talk back, but he wasn't exactly full of sage advice. He wasn't even that great at keeping secrets; he had an uncanny knack for picking up on the words and phrases she most didn't want him to repeat and saying them over and over again. He'd said "Lucy" three times today alone, and each time, she had flashed back to seeing the other woman in her bedroom with Luis. She dreaded to think what he would do with secrets relating to something as important as a murder.

"I wish I'd kept up on journaling," she groaned, resting her elbows on the table and leaning her head into her hands. "At least it would give me a way to vent."

She frowned, remembering something Angela had suggested. Blogging. A travel blog, to be specific. She'd liked the idea, but at the time had thought she would be blogging as herself, something she could share with her friends and family.

But what if she used a screen name and didn't share it with anyone she knew? She could be completely open about *everything* that had happened to her—including winning the lottery, which was quickly beginning to feel like the world's biggest secret to her. She could pour out all of her feelings about finding Tom's body, her worries that one of the people she'd come to know during her stay here might have done it, and she could be honest about her uncertainty going forward. She wouldn't have to keep her happy face on. She wouldn't be risking worrying her parents or giving Luis a road map to her and her winnings. She could just be … her.

Sure, even a blog under a new name might run some risk of being found, but the internet was a big place. It was a chance that she was willing to take. Just the thought of being able to pour her heart out, even if it was to strangers, made her feel lighter, and she got up to fetch her laptop. She wouldn't publish the first post until she left Michigan, just in case, but she could get started on it now.

She woke up the next morning to a shout. Scrambling out of bed, she went to look out the window and saw Angela throwing something at her brother. She tensed, then realized the bright orange thing she'd tossed was just a life jacket. She threw a second one at him from inside the garage, then waved him away. He went to go put them in her car, which already had what looked like other life jackets and some towels in it.

Today was the day they were going boating, and it looked like her companions were eager to head out. She felt a bit bad for not being more excited herself, but the suspicion she had that at least one of them was involved in Tom's death weighed heavily on her, despite the cathartic writing she'd done the night before.

She grabbed a water bottle out of the fridge and wrinkled her nose. A bad smell was hanging in the air, but she couldn't figure out where it was coming from; maybe it was something outside.

Yawning, she turned to Cicero, who was preening himself in his cage. "You wanna go on a boat, bud? I hope you remember all of that training we did with your harness…"

It took some coaxing and one bitten finger, but before too long, she had Cicero in his bright red harness—which was designed specifically for parrots and had a lightweight bungee leash with an end that could either go around her wrist or clip to her belt loop—and she herself was dressed in shorts and a lightweight T-shirt, with her bathing suit on underneath. She grabbed her purse, slipped her feet into her flip-flops, and, with Cicero riding on her shoulder, ventured out to help the others pack for a day on the lake.

Angela's skills at running the diner bled over to organizing for their excursion as well, and it didn't take long before they had everything packed up and ready to go, including a cooler with drinks, sandwiches, and some of Cicero's food. There was a slightly awkward moment when Angela asked if Tulia wanted to ride with them. She made the excuse that she wanted to bring Cicero's travel cage and that there wouldn't be enough room in the car if she squished in with them, but in truth, she just wanted the freedom to drive away if she got a bad feeling about anything.

The drive to the lake didn't take long; the dock where Angela stored her grandmother's boat was just outside of Marquette on Lake Superior and was a quick shot down the main road. It was busy. It seemed a lot of people were taking advantage of the nice Saturday to get out and have fun, but there was plenty of room on the lake for them all. Angela led the way to a medium-sized boat with a small cabin and a collapsible canopy for shade. Benny and Devon set the canopy up while she and Angela loaded the cooler, the towels, and the lifejackets. As she turned around to help Angela lift the cooler into the boat, she glanced out at the parking lot and froze at the sight of a black SUV parked just a few rows away from where they had parked. Her first thought was that it was the two men from the diner … but it couldn't be them. She tried to convince herself that it didn't make sense, that she was just being paranoid, but she was relieved when Angela finally started undoing the rope that tied the boat to the dock and there was still no sign of them.

Before she knew it, she was sitting on a bench seat on board the lovingly named *Rosewater* with Cicero on one hand and her other hand clutching the railing. Angela eased them away from the dock and out onto the lake proper.

The bird seemed uncomfortable with the noise of the engine at first, but once they started moving and the wind hit his feathers, he relaxed and began flapping his wings, trying to pick up some air. His leash was looped securely around her wrist, but she held onto his toes anyway, not wanting him to slip off her hand and get hurt. Devon, who had been uncharacteristically quiet this morning, smiled at the sight.

"Does he think he's flying?"

She laughed. "I don't know. Maybe. He's flown before, but only in the house." Well, and up into a tree just a few days ago, but she didn't want to think of that. She'd come so close to losing him.

"Poor guy. I bet he'd love to just go soaring into the sky."

"Oh, I'm sure he would. It's getting him back that would be the problem. He was hand raised by humans and has zero survival skills; he'd have a good time up there until he landed in a tree, alone, and realized he had no idea where his people were."

Before Devon could respond, Benny flopped down onto the seat between them. "Heyo. Whatcha talking about?"

"I was just asking about her bird," Devon said. He sounded defensive to Tulia, which didn't make any sense. Why would Benny care what he was talking to her about?

"What's his name again?" Benny asked, turning to Tulia.

"Cicero," she said. "My parents named him, supposedly after some old Roman guy, but I think they just liked the name."

"It's better than, like, Spot or something." He stared at the bird, who stared back. "Will he bite me if I try to pet him?"

"Probably." Cicero was usually gentle with her and with her parents—especially her mother—but tended not to like strangers, and especially not men. He might have been small, but his bites were nothing to laugh at.

Benny shrugged and leaned back, eyeing her. "You found Tom with my sister, huh?"

She shifted, noticing that Devon looked just as uncomfortable as she felt. She really didn't want to talk about this now, not on a boat that was already a good half a mile from shore. "Yeah. She asked me to open the lid to the dumpster, and…" Trailing off, she shuddered.

"Well, I'm glad you were there." He lowered his voice, glancing toward the wheel to make sure his sister wasn't paying attention. "I'm glad someone was there with her. It would have been tough for her to handle that alone."

"I think it was pretty bad for both of us," Tulia said, not sure what else to say. "She mentioned she knew him. I'm sure that made it harder for her, and it was hard enough for me even though I'd never seen him before in my life."

"Knew him?" Devon cut in, raising an eyebrow. "She and Tom used to da—" He broke off with an *oof* when Benny elbowed him in the stomach, hard. Both young men got up, Benny glaring daggers at Devon until he walked away. He glanced at Tulia and held her gaze for a second, then forced a smile to his face.

"Hey!" he called out, getting Angela's attention over the wind and the sound of the engine. "We're far enough out, aren't we? Let's drop the anchor and crack some drinks open!"

Tulia stroked the top of Cicero's head idly, watching as Benny and Devon propped the cooler open and Angela cut the engine. There was an air of celebration in the air, but it felt forced, false. As false as the smile that she pasted on her own face.

Something was wrong here, but whatever it was, a mile out onto one of the deepest and largest freshwater lakes in the world wasn't the time or place for her to press the issue.

CHAPTER ELEVEN

The hours they spent on the lake would have been fun at any other time. Tulia felt bad that her smile was strained and that her laughter rang false. Angela had put this outing together for her, and she wished she could just enjoy it like she would have in any other circumstances, but the longer she spent in the company of her companions, the more convinced she became that something was *wrong*. There was an undercurrent to all of their interactions, something that almost felt like suspicion as Angela interacted with her brother, or as Benny and Devon tossed each other a drink without quite looking at each other.

She was relieved when they finally made their way back to shore. By then, she had a headache from the sun and wanted nothing more than to lay in a dark, cool room and rest for a while, but she didn't want to get sucked in to staying for yet another night. As they walked to where they had parked their cars— the SUV was gone, and she still wasn't sure whether the two men from the diner had been in it or not—she gave Angela her best smile.

"I think I'm going to head out when we get back. I don't want to waste too much daylight."

"Oh, are you sure?" Angela asked. "You're welcome to stay another night, if you want."

"I'm sure," Tulia said firmly. "I'm itching to get out of Michigan. I'm excited to see some new places."

"I understand." Angela gave her a small smile as she opened the trunk of her car and heaved the cooler in. "You've got a whole adventure ahead of you."

She settled Cicero into his travel cage and helped the others finish loading up their car, then got into the driver's seat of her own vehicle and started the engine. As they pulled out onto the road, she kept her eyes peeled for the black SUV, but it was nowhere to be seen. Between the men with the SUV and what-ever was going on with Angela and the others, she felt like she was beginning to lose her mind. It would be good to hit the road again, just her, Cicero, and her favorite songs.

Still, she felt a pang as she pulled into Angela's driveway and realized that she'd be saying goodbye for good in a matter of minutes. She wasn't sure if she trusted Angela completely, but she couldn't forget how kind the other woman had been throughout this entire disaster. So much had happened, both positive and negative. Getting away would give her a chance to clear her head.

"Let me put Cicero back in his cage, then I'll help you bring everything in," she offered once they had parked and gotten out of their vehicles.

"Don't worry about it, Benny and Devon can help me. You can focus on getting ready to go. Trash day is Monday, so if you have anything you want to throw away, feel free to toss it in my dumpster. I figure that'll save you a stop somewhere else to do it."

"Thanks," Tulia said with a smile. "I appreciate that."

She let herself into the RV and grabbed an empty garbage bag. Since she hadn't exactly spent much time in it yet, there wasn't very much trash for her to clean out, but she found an empty water bottle to throw away, along with the garbage from when she stopped to get fast food. Then, she went to the fridge and grabbed her leftover pasty. She had completely forgotten about it after her RV was stolen, and while it might still be good, the thought of eating it wasn't exactly appealing, since the person who killed Tom was probably the same one who had been alone in her RV for who knew how long. It probably wasn't very likely that they would have poisoned her food, but she didn't want to risk it.

As she was pulling the bag out of the fridge, the receipt, which had been stuck to the bottom of it, fluttered down to the floor. She shoved the bag with the pasty in it into the garbage bag, then crouched down to pick up the receipt. As she did so, she noticed something white sticking out from under the fridge. It was just the corner of something, and at first, she thought it might be a napkin, or a bit of paper towel, but when she touched the corner that was poking out, she realized it was fabric.

Frowning, she tugged at it. Whatever it was was really shoved under the fridge, so she set the garbage bag down and tugged harder. Finally, it came loose, and as it did, the bad smell she'd noticed in her kitchen that morning grew stronger.

The bundle of fabric unfolded in her hands, and she stared at the dark stain on it. It smelled like blood that had gone bad and stale sweat. It was disgusting, but she couldn't stop staring at it.

The RV had been brand new when she bought it.

There was no way this had been there before. The only explanation for how such a disgusting shirt ended up shoved under the fridge in her RV was that the person who had stolen it had left it there.

It was a man's T-shirt, at least in design. The only question was ... whose? She didn't have any doubts now that the RV thief and the person who had killed Tom were the same person, but she didn't feel any closer to knowing *who* that person was. Samuel and Marc, the mysterious men with the black SUV, might be behind it. They certainly acted oddly enough for it to seem possible, but after the conversation between Angela and the person who had either been her brother or Devon, she'd begun to suspect that it was one of them. The problem was that neither Benny nor Devon had been in the area when Tom was killed. Angela had had to go get them both from Ishpeming that night.

Ishpeming ... where her RV had been found. She didn't know how she hadn't made the connection before, but now it seemed impossible to miss. Had Devon or Benny been at the diner when she first arrived and gotten into a fight with Tom? If one or both of them had been there and were trying to cover up a murder ... did Angela know about it?

She straightened to her feet, feeling sick as she

pinched the shirt in one of the cleaner corners and looked around for somewhere to put it. It might be important DNA evidence, but she didn't want to have to touch it for any longer than she had to.

Someone knocked on the door to the RV. She turned and stared at it, wide-eyed. The last thing she wanted was to talk to any of them, especially with blood-stained evidence literally in her hand. Maybe if she just kept quiet, they would think she was in the bathroom or something and go away.

But then Cicero called out, "Hello? Who is it? Come on in!" in a perfect imitation of her mother's voice … which sounded enough like hers that the person on the other side of the door didn't even hesitate before turning the knob.

Angela stepped up into the RV, a smile on her face that froze, and then fell when she saw Tulia holding the bloody shirt.

CHAPTER TWELVE

"What is that?"

Tulia looked down at the shirt. She considered lying, but only for a second. What lie could she even tell that would be believed?

"It's a bloody shirt. I just found it under my fridge."

They held each other's gaze for a moment, then Angela squeezed her eyes shut. "Oh. Oh, my goodness."

"Angela?"

The other woman shook her head rapidly, as if wanting to deny every word she was hearing. Suddenly, her eyes snapped open. "Are you sure? Are you sure that whoever owned the RV before you didn't leave it behind?"

"I bought the RV new."

The other woman gave a short, sharp laugh. "And you still say you're a waitress. Right." She shook her head. "That doesn't matter now. Can I sit down?"

"Of course."

Angela staggered further into the RV, letting the door fall shut behind her. She walked past Cicero's cage and collapsed onto the built-in sofa.

"I just... I don't understand," she whispered, staring at her hands.

Tulia dropped the shirt onto the crumpled trash bag in front of the fridge. She wasn't throwing it away, but she didn't want to keep holding it. "What's going on, Angela?"

The other woman shook her head. "I don't know."

She narrowed her eyes. "You know something."

Angela took a shuddering breath, looked at the shirt where it lay crumpled on the plastic bag, then burst into tears.

Tulia didn't know what to do. "What—"

Before she could finish asking Angela what was wrong, the other woman stood up and started making her way back toward the RV door. "Sorry, sorry. I just... I can't..." She trailed off with a sob, then pushed her way out of the vehicle.

"Shoot." Tulia hesitated, then grabbed a sheet of

paper towel from the roll she kept on the counter and used it to pinch the shirt between her fingers again without actually touching it. Then, she followed Angela out of the RV. She needed answers.

The other woman had found Devon where he was still unloading the car. He looked befuddled as he patted her shoulder while she cried. Then, he looked up, saw Tulia, and blanched.

"Shoot, Angela, what did you do?" he snapped, grabbing Angela roughly be the shoulder. She tried to pull away, but his grip tightened.

"Hey!" Tulia called out, hurrying forward. Her shout must have alerted him because Benny shoved the door to the house open and stepped out. He spotted Devon manhandling his sister, and his eyes narrowed.

"Dude, what are you doing?" He started toward where they were standing by the car. Devon let go of Angela and spun around to face his friend.

"You're an idiot, Benny."

"What?" Benny stopped in his tracks, looking confused. "What did *I* do? I just put the towels in the washer."

"Not that." Devon glanced back toward Tulia, who was edging toward Angela. She hadn't expected *this.* She'd wanted to talk to the other woman alone, figure out what was going on.

Benny followed his friend's gaze and his eyes fixed on the shirt in Tulia's hands. His eyes rose to meet hers, and then, without another word, he turned around and went back inside.

"Benny!" Angela cried out.

Tulia, finally losing patience with *having no idea what was going on* stepped forward and grabbed the other woman's wrist. "Angela! What's happening? Talk to me."

Angela pulled away. "I can't... I don't understand either. Devon? Whose shirt is that? Please tell me it's yours."

"Benny's an idiot," Devon said in response, sighing. He turned to Tulia. "You shouldn't have gotten involved in this."

Tulia stared down at the shirt in her hands. A man's shirt. She remembered Angela say the night of the murder, "*He was supposed to be here earlier this afternoon,*" about her brother, who she had to go pick up from Ishpeming. The same town her RV had been found just outside of, the same town Devon lived. She remembered her saying "*I knew him. Oh, my goodness, it's Tom. We used to be friends in high school, but he was a jerk, and I stopped seeing him a while ago. I heard he started selling drugs, and he got into a fight with my brother's friend once; I tried to avoid him after that. But he didn't deserve this."*

It was either Benny or Devon, and she thought she knew which it was. She looked up from the shirt to Devon's face, an accusation on the tip of her tongue. Then, Benny came back out of the house, a hunting rifle in his hands, and aimed it at her head.

"No!" Angela jumped in front of her, her arms spread in a shield. "Benny, put that down."

"I can't go to prison, Angela." He moved the rifle slightly, so the barrel wasn't pointing at his sister, but didn't lower it. "We can't trust her not to go to the police."

"Tell me the shirt isn't yours, Benny," Angela said desperately. "It's not you. You didn't kill him. You didn't steal the RV."

Tulia forced herself out of her shock. She'd frozen at the sight of the gun, but now she spoke up. "I think he killed Tom, Angela. You said he was supposed to be at the diner earlier. I think he was. He must have had someone drop him off. But then he ran into Tom before he came in, and after he killed him, he stole my RV as a getaway vehicle and had Devon pick him up by Ishpeming. It's the only thing that makes sense.

He must have hidden his shirt so he wasn't covered in blood when he went into town."

"Benny…" Devon said, his voice full of warning as his friend aimed the rifle. "You're my best friend, man, but I'm not going to cover for you. I said I'd keep quiet over the weekend, give you a chance to talk to your sister and put things in order, but I was never going to keep my mouth shut past Monday. You've got to come clean."

Benny hesitated, then lowered the gun. Angela's voice was broken as she spoke. "They're making things up, right, Benny? You're my little brother. You aren't a murderer."

"It … it wasn't murder," Benny said. He leaned the gun against the porch railing and approached his sister slowly. "It was a fight. Look, I was going to tell you. I swear. I just wanted one last weekend where things were normal."

Angela went to meet him and grabbed his hands with hers. "Just tell me what happened."

He took a deep breath. "I got a friend of mine to drop me off at the diner. I was going to surprise you, which is why I didn't text you when I got there. But then I spotted Tom around the side of the building. Some guy was walking away from him, stuffing a baggie into his pocket, and my blood boiled. I couldn't believe Tom had the gall to be dealing drugs outside of *your* diner. I went to confront him, but he was the one who swung the first punch. It happened so quickly. I dodged and swung back, and he fell and hit his head on the corner of the dumpster. It cut his scalp and he started seizing. There was blood everywhere. I … I panicked. I was worried someone would drive past and see, so I managed to get him into the dumpster, but by then, I had his blood all over me, and I didn't know what to do."

"Why didn't you come into the diner and tell me what happened?"

He gave a dry laugh. "Do you think I wanted to waltz on in there, covered in blood, and say, 'Hey, Angela. Surprise, I'm here! By the way, I think I just killed someone. Will you help me hide the body?'" He shook his head. "I hid out behind the dumpster when I saw Tulia pull up in her RV. When I saw her go in a second time and realized she had left the RV running, I realized that was my chance to get away. I wasn't expecting a bird to freak out and fly at me when I went in, and I felt bad when I realized I'd let someone's pet escape, but I didn't have time to stop or to change my mind. I took off down the road to Ishpeming and told Devon I needed his help. I wasn't expecting you to find the body."

"I got the story out of him when I picked him up, shirtless, outside of a stolen RV," Devon said. "For some reason, he thought I wouldn't question any of that. I tried to tell you, Angela."

"I know," she whispered. She looked at Benny, squeezed his hands, and then stepped back. "Go inside. I just… I need a minute. Then, we're going to call the police and get this straightened out."

Benny just nodded, sighing heavily as he turned and trudged back towards the door, bypassing the rifle. Devon hesitated, then followed him.

Angela turned to Tulia. "I'm so sorry."

"You're sorry?" Tulia blinked. "For what?"

"For all of this. I can't believe he pointed a gun at you. I … I had my suspicions, especially when Devon tried to tell me something was going on, but I just couldn't believe he would actually kill someone."

"It's not your fault." Tulia went to hug her, realized she was still holding the bloody shirt, and let her arms fall to her side. Angela gave her a weak smile.

"No, but I should have listened to my gut." She sighed. "It looks like you'll have to stay longer after all. I'm sure the police will want to talk to you too."

"I'll stay as long as you need me to," Tulia promised. It was the least she could do.

EPILOGUE

Tulia set the RV's cruise control and then reached over to crank the radio louder. In his cage in the passenger seat beside her, Cicero started bobbing his head. She grinned and joined him, nodding along to the music.

The highway stretched out in front of her. Behind her, Marquette, Ishpeming, and everyone she had met during the first, chaotic week of her trip were slowly falling farther and farther away.

Ever since she bought that lottery ticket, the highs and lows in her life seemed to have changed from hills and valleys to mountains and canyons. This first leg of her trip had been no different. She'd had a great time, except for the times when she'd had a horrible time, and there really hadn't been much in between.

She wasn't sure what sentencing Benny would get for what had happened. He'd gone willingly with the police, and Angela was already looking into a lawyer for him. Even with the best lawyer in the world, though, Tulia was sure it would be a long time before he saw the outside of a jail cell again.

Somehow, Angela didn't blame her for any of it, even though she had been the one to uncover the final, unignorable piece of evidence when she found the shirt he had hidden in the RV. Against the odds, Tulia had the feeling she had made a lifelong friend. In fact, as of right now, Angela was the only reader her new blog had … and was the only one, other than her parents, who knew about the winning lottery ticket that had changed her life. She'd known that letting the other woman read her blog would give her secret away, but after all they had been through, it had felt right, and she didn't regret it yet.

And now, she was finally moving on. She was still in Michigan but would be reaching Wisconsin in a matter of hours, where she was planning to camp—at an actual campground this time—and hit some nature trails before seeing what else the neighboring state had to offer.

As she drove, she occasionally glanced in the side mirror at the traffic behind her. She wasn't sure, but she thought she saw a black SUV a few cars behind her. It might not be Samuel and Marc's vehicle. For all she knew, it would turn off the highway in a few miles, and she would never see it again. But somehow, she got the feeling that she hadn't seen the last of those men yet. They might not have killed Tom, but they were certainly up to something. She would just have to hope that she could handle whatever happened. And for the first time in a long time, she was beginning to feel confident that she could handle anything life threw at her.

Made in the USA
Coppell, TX
22 September 2023

21900853R00066